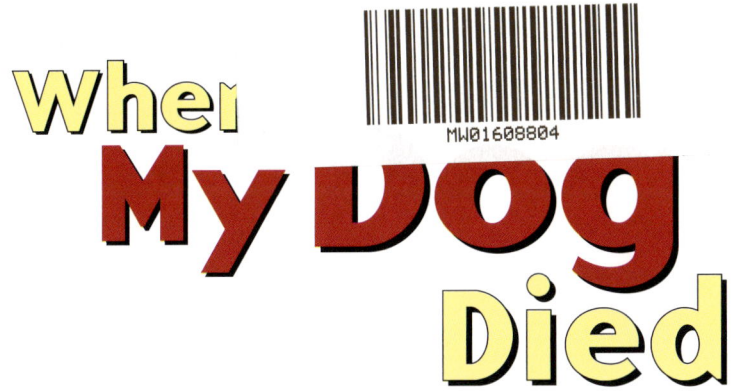

When My Dog Died

Julia Wall

illustrated by Martin Bailey

 Learning Media®

My dog, Banjo, and I did lots of things
together. The two of us went for walks,
visited friends, and watched TV.
Sometimes my older brother took
us in his car to the park, where we'd
toss a ball for Banjo to chase.

Banjo died when he was ten years old,
which is quite a good age for a dog.
I cried for a whole morning. Banjo was
one of my best buddies, and I couldn't
believe how lonely I felt without him.

It took me a while to get used to not having Banjo around, and I cried a lot at first. Sometimes I'd forget that he was dead and wonder where he was.

My brother told me it was OK to cry when I was feeling sad about Banjo.

After a bit, I started to feel angry – it seemed so unfair that Banjo was dead. There were times when I didn't want to believe that he was gone.

When I talked to Mom about how I was feeling, she said it was natural to feel upset, angry even. After all, death is a pretty big deal. She gave me hugs when I was feeling upset about losing Banjo.

For a while after Banjo died, I didn't know what to do with myself. I didn't feel like going to see friends, watching TV, or going to the park. I just felt like being on my own.

Sometimes I'd see someone on the street walking a dog that looked a lot like Banjo.

Seeing them reminded me about all the walks that Banjo and I had taken around the neighborhood, and I'd start missing him again.

I used to dream about Banjo after he'd died, and I still do sometimes. In my dreams, we're having fun together. When I wake up and realize my dreams aren't true, I feel sad all over again.

When I'm sad, I talk about how I feel with Mom. She reminds me about the funny things my dog did, like hiding under the car seat when we went to the park.

Now I think about Banjo less than I did when he first died. I guess I'm getting used to the idea that he isn't around, but that doesn't mean I've forgotten him. There's no way that will happen!

I've kept some of Banjo's things, like his leash and basket. They help me to remember him and, who knows, one day, I might get a new dog.

If I do get a new dog, that won't mean I've stopped loving Banjo. No way! It will just mean I'll have a new dog to watch TV with and to take for walks.